♥ p u p p y & m e

Breakfast Time

MW00752127

by Julia Noonan

Cartwheel
B·O·O·K·S ®

SCHOLASTIC INC.

New York Toronto London Auckland Sydney Mexico City New Delhi Hong Kong

Here's my bib, and
   here's my spoon.
Food is coming
   very soon!
Puppy barks a
   breakfast tune.

We both sing for breakfast.

Mommy! Look what
we can do!
I use toast for
peek-a-boo.
Then I eat it.
Pup does, too.

Crunchy, munchy breakfast.

Now I drop my
favorite cup!
Juice spills on the
floor near Pup.
I watch Puppy
lick it up!

Puppy cleans at breakfast.

I make corn flakes
fall like snow.
Puppy watches
from below.
Catches every one
I throw!

Puppy's fast at breakfast.

Puppy dances!
Then he begs.
Then he helps me
eat my eggs.
He licks yogurt
off my legs.

Tickle-time at breakfast.

Mommy takes my
bowl and cup.
Giant washcloth
cleans us up.
I am full, and
so is Pup!

Tummies full of breakfast.

New clothes come when
food is done.
Time for Pup and
me to run!
Find a morning
full of fun.

Now that we've had breakfast.

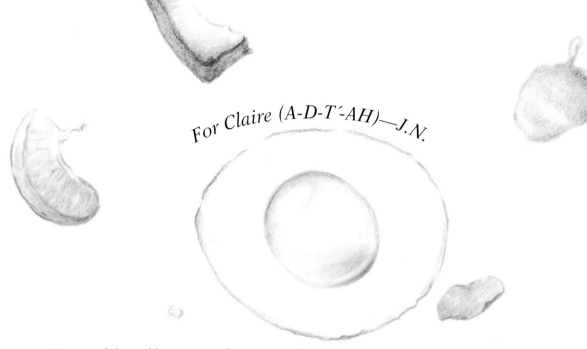

For Claire (A-D-T'-AH)—J.N.

ISBN 0-439-11490-X

Copyright © 2000 by Julia Noonan.
All rights reserved. Published by Scholastic Inc.
SCHOLASTIC, CARTWHEEL BOOKS and associated logos are trademarks and/or registered trademarks of Scholastic Inc.

12 11 10 9 8 7 6 5 4 3 2 1   0/0 01 02 03 04 05

Printed in Malaysia   46
First printing, June 2000

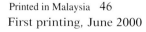